Swan

Also by Jane Gardam

BRIDGET & WILLIAM
HORSE
(*Blackbirds*)

KIT
KIT IN BOOTS
(*Redwings*)

Swan

Jane Gardam

Illustrated by John Dillow

Julia MacRae Books
A division of Franklin Watts

Text © 1987 Jane Gardam
Illustrations © 1987 John Dillow
All rights reserved
First published in Great Britain 1987 by
Julia MacRae Books
A division of Franklin Watts
12a Golden Square, London W1R 4BA
and Franklin Watts, Australia,
14 Mars Road, Lane Cove, NSW 2066

British Library Cataloguing in Publication Data
Gardam, Jane
Swan──(Redwing books)
I. Title
823'.914[J]   PZ7
ISBN 0 86203 263 6

Phototypeset by Ace Filmsetting Ltd, Frome, Somerset
Printed and bound in Great Britain by
Garden City Press, Letchworth

Contents

Chapter One

Two boys walked over the bridge.

They were big boys from the private school on the rich side of the river. One afternoon each week they had to spend helping people. They helped old people with no-one to love them and younger children who were finding school difficult. It was a rule.

"I find school difficult myself," said Jackson. "Exams for a start."

"I have plenty of people at home who think no-one loves them," said Pratt. "Two grand-parents, two parents, one sister."

"And all called Pratt, poor things," said Jackson, and he and Pratt began to fight in a

friendly way, bumping up against each other
until Jackson fell against a lady with a
shopping-trolley on a stick and all her
cornflakes fell out and a packet of flour, which
burst.

"I'm going straight to your school," she said. "I know that uniform. It's supposed to be a good school. I'm going to lay a complaint," and she wagged her arms up and down at the elbows like a hen. Pratt, who often found words coming out of his mouth without warning said, "Lay an egg. Cluck, cluck."

"That's done it. That's finished it," said the woman. "I'm going right round now. *And* I'll say you were slopping down the York Road Battersea at two o'clock in the afternoon, three miles from where you ought to be."

"We are doing our Social Work," said Pratt. "Helping people."

"Helping people," said the woman, pointing at the pavement.

"We're being interviewed to take care of unfortunate children," said Jackson.

"They're unfortunate all right if all they can get is you." And she steamed off, leaving the flour spread about like snow, and passers-by walked over it giving dark looks and taking ghostly footprints away into the distance. Pratt eased as much of it as he could into the gutter with his feet.

"She's right," he said. "I don't know much about unfortunate children. Or any children."

"They may not let us when they see us," said Jackson. "Come on. We'd better turn up. They can look at us and form an opinion."

Chapter Two

"Whatever's that mess on your shoes?" asked
the Head Teacher at the school on the rough
side of the river, coming towards them across
the hall. "Dear me, snow. It *is* a nasty day. How
do you do? Your children are ready for you, I
think. Maybe today you might like just to talk
to them indoors and start taking them out next
week?"

"Yes, please," said Jackson.

"Taking them *out*?" said Pratt.

"Yes. The idea is that – with the parents'
consent – you take them out and widen their
lives. Most of them on this side of the river
never go anywhere. It's a depressed area.

11

Their lives are simply school (or truanting), television, bed and school, though we have children from every country in the world."

"It's about the same for us," said Pratt. "Just cross out television and insert homework."

"Oh, come now," said the Head Teacher, "you do lots of things. Over the river, there's the Zoo and all the museums and the Tower of London and all the lovely shops. All the good things happen over the bridge. Most of our children here have scarcely seen a blade of grass. Now – you are two very reliable boys, I gather?" (She looked a bit doubtful.) "Just wipe your feet and follow me."

She opened a door of a classroom, but there was silence inside and only one small Chinese boy looking closely into the side of a fish-tank.

"Dear me. Whatever . . . ? Oh, of course. They're all in the gym. This is Henry. Henry Wu. He doesn't do any team-games. Or – anything, really. He is one of the children you are to try to help. Now which of you would like Henry? He's nearly seven."

12

"I would," said Pratt, wondering again why words kept emerging from his mouth.

"Good. I'll leave you here then. Your friend and I will go and find the other child. Come here Henry and meet – what's your name?"

"Pratt."

"Pratt. HERE'S PRATT, HENRY. He's not deaf, Pratt. Or dumb. He's been tested. It is just that he won't speak or listen. He shuts himself away. PRATT, HENRY," she said, and vanished with an ushering arm behind Jackson, closing the door.

Henry Wu watched the fish.

13

Chapter Three

"Hello," said Pratt after a while. "Fish."

He thought, that is a very silly remark. He made it again, "Fish."

The head of Henry Wu did not move. It was a small round head with thick hair, black and shiny as the feathers on the diving-ducks in the park across the river.

Or it might have been the head of a doll. A very fragile Chinese-china doll. Pratt walked round it to try and get a look at the face on the front which was creamy-coloured with a nose so small it hardly made a bump, and leaf-shaped eyes with no eye-lashes. No, not leaf-shaped, pod-shaped, thought Pratt, and in each pod the blackest and most glossy berry which looked at the fish. The fish opened their mouths at the face in an anxious manner and waved their floaty tails about.

"What they telling you?" asked Pratt. "Friends of yours are they?"

Henry Wu said nothing.

"D'you want to go and see the diving-ducks in our park?"

Henry Wu said nothing.

"Think about it," said Pratt. "Next week. It's a good offer."

Henry Wu said nothing.

"Take it or leave it."

Pratt wondered for a moment if the Chinese boy was real. Maybe he was a sort of waxwork. If you gave him a push maybe he'd just tip over and fall on the floor. "Come on, Henry Wu," he said. "Let's hear what you think," and he gave the boy's shoulder a little shove.

And found himself lying on the floor with no memory of being put there. He was not at all hurt – just lying. And the Chinese boy was still

sitting on his high stool looking at the fish.

Pandemonium was approaching along the passage and children of all kinds began to hurtle in. They all stopped in a huddle when they saw large Pratt spread out over the floor, and a teacher rushed forward. The Head Teacher and Jackson were there, too, at the back, and Jackson was looking surprised.

"Oh dear," said the teacher, "his mother taught him to fight in case he was bullied. She's a Black Belt in judo. She told us he was very good at it. Oh Henry – not again. This big boy wants to be kind to you."

"All I said," said Pratt, picking himself up, "was that I'd take him to the diving-ducks in the park. What's more, I shall," he added, glaring at Henry Wu.

"Why bother?" said Jackson. They were on their way home. "He looks a wimp. He looks a rat. I don't call him unfortunate. I call him unpleasant."

"What was yours like?"

"Mine wasn't. She'd left. She was a fairground child. They're always moving on. The school seems a bit short of peculiar ones at the moment. I'll share Henry Wu the Great Kung Fu with you if you like. You're going to need a bit of protection by the look of it."

Chapter Four

But in the end Jackson didn't, for he was given an old lady's kitchen to paint and was soon spending his Wednesdays and all his free time in it, eating her cooking. Pratt set out the following week to the school alone and found Henry Wu waiting for him, muffled to just below the eyebrows in a fat grasshopper cocoon of bright red nylon padding.

"Come on," said Pratt and without looking to see if Henry followed, set out along the grim York Road to a bus-stop. Henry climbed on the bus behind him and sat some distance away, glaring at space.

"One and a half to the park," said Pratt,

taking out a French grammar book. They made an odd pair. Pratt put on dark glasses in case he met friends.

It was January. The park was cold and dead. The grass was mothy and muddy and full of puddly places and nobody in the world could feel the better for seeing a blade of it. Plants were sticks. There were no birds yet about the trees, and the water in the lake and round the

little island was heavy and dark and still, like
forgotten soup.

The kiosk café was shut up. The metal tables
and chairs of summer were stacked inside and
the coke machine was empty. Pigeons walked
near the kiosk, round and round on the cracked

tarmac. They were as dirty and colourless as everything else but Henry looked at them closely as they clustered round his feet. One bounced off the ground and landed on his head.

Henry did not laugh or cry out or jump, but stood.

"Hey, knock that off. It's filthy," shouted Pratt. "They're full of diseases, London

22

pigeons. Look at their knuckles – all bleeding and rotten.''

A large black-and-white magpie came strutting by and regarded Henry Wu with the pigeon on his head. The pigeon flew away. Henry Wu began to follow the magpie along the path.

''It's bad luck, one magpie,'' said Pratt, ''one for sorrow, two for joy,'' and at once a second magpie appeared, walking behind. The Chinese boy walked in procession between the two magpies under the bare trees.

''Come on. It's time to go,'' said Pratt, feeling jealous. The magpies flew away and they went to catch the bus.

Chapter Five

Every Wednesday of that cold winter term, Pratt took Henry Wu to the park, walking up and down with his French book or his Science book open before him while Henry watched the birds and said nothing.

"Has he *never* said anything?" he asked the Head Teacher. "I suppose he talks Chinese at home?"

"No. He doesn't say a thing. There's someone keeping an eye on him of course. A Social Worker. But the parents don't seem to be unduly worried. His home is very Chinese, I believe. The doctors say that one day he should begin to speak, but maybe not for years. We have to be patient."

"Has he had some bad experiences? Is he a Boat Person?"

"No. He is just private. He is a village boy from China. Do you want to meet his family? You ought to. They ought to meet you, too. It will be interesting for you. Meeting Chinese."

"There are Chinese at our school."

"Millionaires' sons from Hong Kong I expect, with English as their first language. This will be more exciting. These people have chosen to come and live in England. They are immigrants."

"I'm going to meet some immigrants," said Pratt to Jackson. "D'you want to come?"

"No," said Jackson to Pratt, "I'm cleaning under Nellie's bed where she can't reach. And I'm teaching her to use a calculator."

"Isn't she a bit old for a calculator?"

"She likes it. Isn't it *emi*grants?"

"No, immigrants. Immigrants come *in* to a country."

"Why isn't it innigrants then?"

"I don't know. Latin I expect if you look it

up. Emigrants are people who go out of a country.''

''Well, haven't these Chinese come out of a country? As well as come in to a country? They're emigrants and immigrants. They don't know whether they're coming or going. Perhaps that's what's the matter with Henry Wu.''

''Henry's not an innigrant. He's a *ninny*grant. Or just plain *ig*norant. I'm sick of him if you want to know. It's a waste of time, my Social Work. At least you get some good food out of yours. You've started her cooking again. And you're teaching her about machines.''

''Your Chinese will know about machines. I shouldn't touch the food, though, if you go to them. It won't be like a Take-away.''

''D'you want to come?''

''No thanks. See you.''

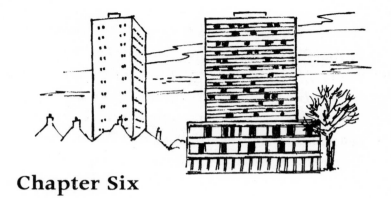

Chapter Six

"Candlelight Mansions," said the Social Worker. "Here we are. Twelfth floor and the lifts won't be working. I hope you're fit."

They climbed the concrete stairs. Rubbish lay about. People had scrawled ugly things on the walls. On every floor the lift had a board saying OUT OF ORDER hung across it with chains. Most of the chains were broken, too, so that the boards hung crooked. All was silent.

Then, as they walked more slowly up the final flights of stairs, the silence ceased. Sounds began to be threaded into it: thin, busy sounds that became more persistent as they turned at the twelfth landing and met a fluttery excited

27

chorus. Across the narrow space were huge heaps. Bundles and crates and boxes were stacked high under tarpaulins with only the narrowest of alleys left to lead up to the splintery front door of Henry Wu's flat. A second door of diamonds of metal was fastened across this. Nailed to the wall, on top of all the bundles were two big makeshift bird cages like sideways chicken-houses and inside them, dozens of birds – red and blue and green and yellow making as much noise as a school playground.

"Oh dear," said the Social Worker, "here we go again. The Council got them all moved once but the Wus just put them back. They pretend they don't understand. Good afternoon, Mrs Wu."

A beautiful, flat Chinese lady had come to the door and stood behind the metal diamonds. She did not look in the least like a Black Belt in judo. She was very thin and small and wore

29

bedroom slippers, a satin dress and three cardigans. She bowed.

"I've just called for a chat and to bring you Henry's kind friend who is trying to help him."

Mrs Wu took out a key and then clattered back the metal gate and smiled and bowed a great deal and you couldn't tell what she was thinking. From the flat behind her there arose the most terrible noise of wailing, screeching and whirring, and Pratt thought that Jackson had been right about machines. A smell wafted out, too. A sweetish, dryish, spicy smell which sent a long thrill down Pratt's spine. It smelled of far, far away.

"You have a great many belongings out here," said the Social Worker climbing over a great many more as they made their way down the passage into the living-room. In the living-room were more again, and an enormous Chinese family wearing many layers of clothes and sitting sewing among electric fires. Two electric sewing-machines whizzed and a tape of Chinese music plinked and wailed, full-tilt.

Another, different tape wailed back through
the open kitchen door where an old lady was
gazing into steaming pans on a stove. There
were several bird cages hanging from hooks, a
fish tank by the window and a rat-like object

looking out from a bundle of hay in a cage. It had one eye half-shut as if it had a headache. Henry Wu was regarding this rat.

The rest of the family all fell silent, rose to their feet and bowed. "Hello Henry," said Pratt, but Henry did not look round, even when his mother turned her sweet face on him and sang out a tremendous Chinese torrent.

Tea came in glasses. Pratt sat and drank his as the Social Worker talked to Mrs Wu and the other ladies, and a small fat Chinese gentleman, making little silk buttons without even having to watch his hands, watched Pratt. After a time he shouted something and a girl came carrying a plate. On the plate were small grey eggs with a skin on them. She held them out to Pratt.

"Hwile," said the Chinese gentleman, his needle stitching like magic. "Kwile."

"Oh yes," said Pratt. (Whale?)

"Eat. Eat."

"I'm not very . . ."

But the Social Worker glared. "Quail," she said.

32

"Eggs don't agree . . ." said Pratt. (Aren't quails, snakes?). He imagined a tiny young snake curled inside each egg. I'd rather die, he thought, and saw that for the first time Henry Wu was looking at him from his corner. So was the rat.

So were the fish, the birds, Mrs Wu, the fat gentleman and all the assorted aunts. He ate the egg which went down *glup*, like an oval leather pill. Everyone smiled and nodded and the plate was offered again.

He ate another egg and thought, two snakes. They'll breed. I will die. He took a great swig of tea and smiled faintly. Everyone in the room then, except the rat, the fish and Henry, began to laugh and twitter and talk. The old woman slipper-sloppered in from the kitchen bringing more things to eat in dolls' bowls. They were filled with little chippy things and spicy, hot juicy bits. She pushed them at Pratt. "Go on," said the Social Worker. "Live dangerously."

Pratt ate. Slowly at first. It was delicious. "It's not a bit like the Take-Away," he said,

eating faster. This made the Chinese laugh.
"Take-Away, Take-Away," they said. "Sweet-
and-Sour," said Mrs Wu. "Not like Sweet-and-
Sour," and everyone made tut-tutting noises
which meant, "I should just hope not." Mrs Wu
then gave Pratt a good-luck charm made of
brass and nodded at him as if she admired him.

"She's thanking you for taking Henry out,"
said the Social Worker as they went down all
the stairs again.

"She probably thinks I'm a lunatic," said

Pratt, "taking Henry out. Much good it's done."

"You don't know yet."

"Well, he's not exactly talking is he? Or doing anything. He's probably loopy. She probably thinks I'm loopy, too."

"She wouldn't let you look after him if she thought you were loopy."

"Maybe she wants rid of him. She's hoping I'll kidnap him. I'm not looking after him any more if he can't get up and say hello. Or even smile. After all those terrible afternoons. Well, I've got exams next term. I've got no time. I'll have to think of myself all day and every day from now on, thank goodness.''

And the next term it was so. Pratt gave never a thought to Henry Wu except sometimes when the birds began to be seen about the school gardens again and to swoop under the eaves of the chapel. Swallows, he thought, immigrants. And he remembered him when his parents took him out to a Chinese restaurant on his birthday.

"Oh no – not those," he said.

"They are the greatest Chinese treat you can have," said his father. "Quails' eggs."

"Aren't they serpents?"

"Serpents? Don't you learn *any* general knowledge at that school? They're birds' eggs. Have some Sweet-and-Sour."

"The Chinese don't have Sweet-and-Sour. It was made up for the tourists."

"Really? Where did you hear that?"

"My Social Work."

Chapter Seven

The exams came and went as exams do and Pratt felt light-headed and light-hearted. He came out of the last one with Jackson and said, "Whee – let's go and look at the river."

"I feel great. Do you?" he said.

Jackson said he felt terrible. He'd failed everything. He'd spent too much time spring-cleaning old Nellie. He knew he had.

"I expect I've failed, too," said Pratt, but he felt he hadn't. The exams had been easy. He felt very comfortable and pleased with himself and watched the oily river sidle by, this way and that way, slopping up against the arches of the bridge, splashy from the barges. "What

shall we do?'' he asked Jackson. "Shall we go
on the river?''

"I'd better go over and see if old Nellie's in,''
said Jackson. "I promised. Sorry. You go.''

Pratt stood for a while and the old lady with
the shopping-trolley went by. "Lolling about,''
she said.

"I'm sorry about your flour," said Pratt. Filled with happiness because the exams were over he felt he ought to be nice to the woman.

But she hurried on. Pratt watched her crossing the bridge and found his feet following. He made for Candlelight Mansions.

"Does Henry want to come to the park?" he asked a little girl who peered through the diamonds. Her face was like a white violet and her fringe was flimsy as a paint-brush. There was a kerfuffle behind her and Mrs Wu came forward to usher him inside.

If I go in it'll be quails' eggs and hours of bowing, thought Pratt. "I'll wait here," he said firmly. Mrs Wu disappeared and after a time Henry was produced, again muffled to the nose in the scarlet padding.

"It's pretty warm out," said Pratt, but Mrs Wu only nodded and smiled.

In the park Pratt felt lost without a book and Henry marched wordlessly, as far ahead as possible. The ice-cream kiosk was open now and people sitting on the metal chairs. Pigeons

41

clustered round them in flustery clouds.

"Horrible," said Pratt, catching up with Henry. "Rats with wings. I'll get you a coke but we'll drink it over there by the grass – hey! Where you going?"

Henry, not stopping for the pigeons, was away to the slope of green grass that led down

to the water. On the grass and all over the water was a multitude of birds and all the ducks of the park, diving-ducks and pelicans and geese and dab-chicks and water-hens and mallards. Old ducks remembering and new little ducks being shown the summer for the first time. Some of the new ducks were so new they were still covered with fluff – white fluff, fawn fluff, yellow fluff and even black fluff, like decorations on a hat. The proud parent ducks had large V's of water rippling out behind them and small V's rippled behind all the following babies. Henry Wu stood still.

Then round the island on the lake there came a huge, drifting meringue.

It was followed by another, but this one had a long neck sweeping up from it with a proud head on the end and a brilliant orange beak and two black nostrils, the shape of Henry Wu's eyes.

The first meringue swelled and fluffed itself and a tall neck and wonderful head emerged from that one, too.

43

Suddenly Henry pointed a short padded arm
at these amazing things and keeping it stiff
turned his face up to Pratt and looked at him
very intently.

"Swan," said Pratt. "They're swans. They're
all right, aren't they? Hey – but don't do that.
They're not so all right that you ought to get
near them."

"Get that boy back," shouted a man. "They'll
knock him down. They're fierce, them two."

"Nasty things, swans," said someone else.

But Henry was off, over the little green
hooped fence, running, running at the swans as
they stepped out of the water on their black
macintosh feet and started up the slope
towards him. They lowered their necks and
began to hiss. They opened their great wings.

"Oh help," said Pratt.

"It's all right," said the man. "I'm the
Warden. I'll get him. Skin him alive, too, if they

don't do it first," and he ran down the slope.

But the swans did not skin Henry Wu alive. As he ran right up to them they stopped. They turned their heads away as if they were thinking. They shifted from one big black leathery foot to another and stopped hissing. Then they opened their wings wider still and dropped them gently and carefully back in place. They had a purple band round each left leg. One said 888. White swans, purple bands,

orange beaks, red Henry Wu, all on the green grass with the water and the willows about them all sparkling and swaying.

"Bless him – isn't that nice now?" said the crowd, as the Warden of the swans gathered up

Henry and brought him back under his arm.
"You'll get eaten one day," said the Warden,
"you'll go getting yourself harmed," but he
seemed less angry than he might.

On the way home Henry did not look at Pratt
but sat with him on the long seat just inside the
bus. It was a seat for three people and Henry
sat as far away as possible. But it was the same
seat.

Chapter Eight

Then Pratt went on his summer holidays and when he came back the exam results were out and they were not marvellous. He stuffed miserably about in the house. When Jackson called – Jackson had done rather well – he said that he was busy, which he wasn't.

But he made himself busy the next term, stodging glumly along, and took the exams all over again.

"Are you going to see your Chinese Demon any more?" asked Jackson afterwards. "Come and meet old Nellie."

"No thanks."

"She says to bring you."

"No thanks."

But when the results came out this time, they were very good. He had more than passed.

Pratt said, "How's Nellie?"

"Oh fine. Much better tempered."

"Was she bad tempered? You never said."

"How's Henry Wu? Did you ever get him talking?"

"No. He was loopy."

But it was a fine frosty day and the sun for the moment was shining and Pratt went to the park and over the grass to the lakeside where one of the swans came sliding around the island and paddled about on the slope, marking time and looking at him.

It dazzled. The band round his leg said 887. "Where's your husband?" said Pratt. "Or wife or whatever? Are you hungry or something?"

The sun went in and the bare trees rattled. The swan looked a bit lonely and he thought he might go and get it some bread. Instead he took a bus back over the bridge and went to Candlelight Mansions.

50

They've probably forgotten me, he thought
as he rang the bell. The bundles and the bird
cages had gone from the landing. He rattled the
steel mesh. They've probably moved, he
thought, they've gone back to China.

51

But he was welcomed like a son.

"Can I take Henry out?"

Bowings, grinnings, buttonings-up of Henry
who had not grown one millimetre.

"Where's the rat?" Pratt asked.

"Nwee-sance," said Mrs Wu.

"Neeoo-sance," said the fat gentleman.
"Nee-oosance. Council told them go."

But the flat was now a jungle of floating paper-kites and plants with scarlet dragons flying about in them, mixed with Father Christmasses, Baby Jesuses and strings of Christmas tinsel. In the kitchen the old lady stirred the pots to a radio playing *Oh Come all ye Faithful*. Henry, seeing everyone talking together sat down under a sewing-machine.

"Has he said anything yet?" asked Pratt, eating juicy bits with chopsticks. Everyone watched the juicy bits falling off the chopsticks and laughed. Now and then, when anything reached his mouth successfully, they congratulated him. They ignored the question, which meant that Henry had not.

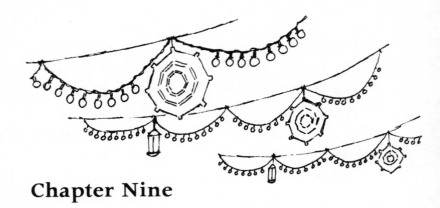

Chapter Nine

It was cold in the street and very cold as they
stood at the bus stop. Pratt had forgotten that
the days were now so short, and already it was
beginning to get dark. Far too late to go to the
park, he thought. The bus was cold, too, and
dirty, and all the people looked as if they'd like
to be warm at home in bed. "Come on – we'll go
upstairs and sit in the front," said Pratt and
they looked down on the dreary York Road
with all its little shops and, now and then, a
string of coloured Christmas lights across it
with half the bulbs broken or missing. Some
shops had spray-snowflakes squirted on the
windows. It looked like cleaning-fluid someone

54

had forgotten to wash off. Real snowflakes were beginning to fall and looked even dingier than the shop-window ones.

I should have taken him over the river to see some real Christmas lights in Regent Street, thought Pratt. There's nothing over here.

But there came a bang.

A sort of rushing, blustering, flapping before the eyes.

The glass in the window in front of them rattled like an earthquake and something fell down in front of the bus.

There were screeching brakes and shouting people and Pratt and Henry were flung forward on to the floor.

As they picked themselves up they saw people running into the road below. "Something fell out of the sky," said Pratt to Henry Wu. "Something big. Like a person."

But it was not a person. It was a swan that sat heavy and large and streaked with a dark mark across its trailing wings in the very middle of the road.

"Swan, swan – it's a swan!" everybody was shouting. "It's killed itself. It's dead. Frozen dead with fright."

"It hit a wire," said someone else – it was the lady with the shopping-trolley – "I saw it. An overhead-wire from the lights. They oughtn't to be allowed. They're not worth it. They could have electrocuted that bus."

"It's killed it, anyway," said Jackson, who seemed to be with her. "It's stone dead."

But the swan was not dead. Suddenly it decided it was not. It heaved up its head and wings and lollopped itself to the side of the road and flopped down again, looking round slowly, with stunned wonder, opening and shutting its orange beak, though with never a sound.

"It was migrating," said a man from a chip shop.

"Swans don't migrate, they stay put," said a man from a laundry.

"Anyone'd migrate this weather," said a man selling whelks and eels. "Look, it's got a number on it. It's from the park. Look, it's put itself all tidy on the yellow line."

"Out of the way," said a policeman. "Now then. Stand aside. We'll want a basket." A laundry basket was brought and someone lent the policeman a strong pair of gloves.

"Clear a space," he said and approached the swan which proved it was not dead by landing the policeman a thwacking blow with its wing.

"Have to be shot," said a dismal man from a bike shop. "Well, it's no chicken."

"Course it's no chicken," said the woman with the trolley. "If it was a chicken it'd be coming home with me and a bag of chips."

And then a girl with purple hair began to shriek and scream because she didn't believe in eating animals, which included birds.

"Anyway, all swans belong to the Queen," said the trolley lady. "I heard it on Gardener's Question Time."

"I'm going crazy," said the policeman who had withdrawn to a little distance to talk into his radio-set. "If they all belong to the Queen I hope she'll come and collect this one. I'm not sure I can. Move along now. We have to keep the traffic moving. We can't hold up London for a swan."

One or two cars sidled by, but otherwise nobody moved. It was a strange thing. In the middle of the dead dark day and the dead dark street sat the open laundry basket and the

shining, mute bird with its angel feathers. The
road fell quiet.

Then Henry Wu stepped forward, small
inside his padding, and put small arms round

the bulk of the swan's back and lifted it lightly
into the basket where it fluffed up its feathers
like rising bread and gazed round proudly at
the people.

"Heaven on high!" said everyone. "The
weight!"

"His mother's a Black Belt," said Pratt
proudly.

"That Chinese'll have to be washed," said the

trolley lady. "They'd better both come home with us, Jackson, and I'll give them their tea."

But Pratt and Henry did not go home with old Nellie on that occasion because the policeman asked them to go back to the station with him and the swan. If Henry would be so kind as to assist him, he said. And Henry stroked the swan's docile head twice and then folded it down with its neck behind it – and a

big strong neck it was, though very arrangeable
– and quickly put down the lid.

The Park Warden came to the police station
and he and Henry and Pratt and the swan went
to the park where the swan took to the water
like a whirlwind and faded in to the dark.

"Off you go, 888," said the Warden. "There's
your missis to meet you. You wouldn't have
seen her again if you'd not dropped among
friends."

"They can't take off, you see," he said to the
two boys, "except on water. They're like the
old sea-planes."

Pratt watched the two white shapes fade
with the day. "They're strange altogether,
swans," said the Warden. "Quite silent!"

"Is it true they sing when they're dying?"
asked Pratt. "I read it. In poetry."

"Well, that one's not dying then," said the
Warden. "Gone without a sound. Means all's
well. It's funny – most living creatures make
some sort of a noise to show they're happy.
Goodbye, Henry. There'll be a job for you with

creatures one day. I dare say when you grow up you'll get my job. You have the touch.''

On the bus back over the bridge to Candlelight Mansions Henry sat down next to Pratt on a double seat and staring in front of him said in a high, clear Chinese-English voice, ''Hwan.''

''Hwan,'' he said. ''Hwan, hwan, hwan, swan. Swan, swan, SWAN,'' until Pratt had to say, ''Shut up Henry or they'll think you're loopy.''